This
Funny Jokes Book
Belongs To

____

____

Knock, knock.
Who's there?
Wet.
Wet who?
Wet me in, it's raining
out here!

Q: What do you call a dinosaur that is sleeping?
A: dino-snore!

Q: What is fast, loud and crunchy?
A: A rocket chip!

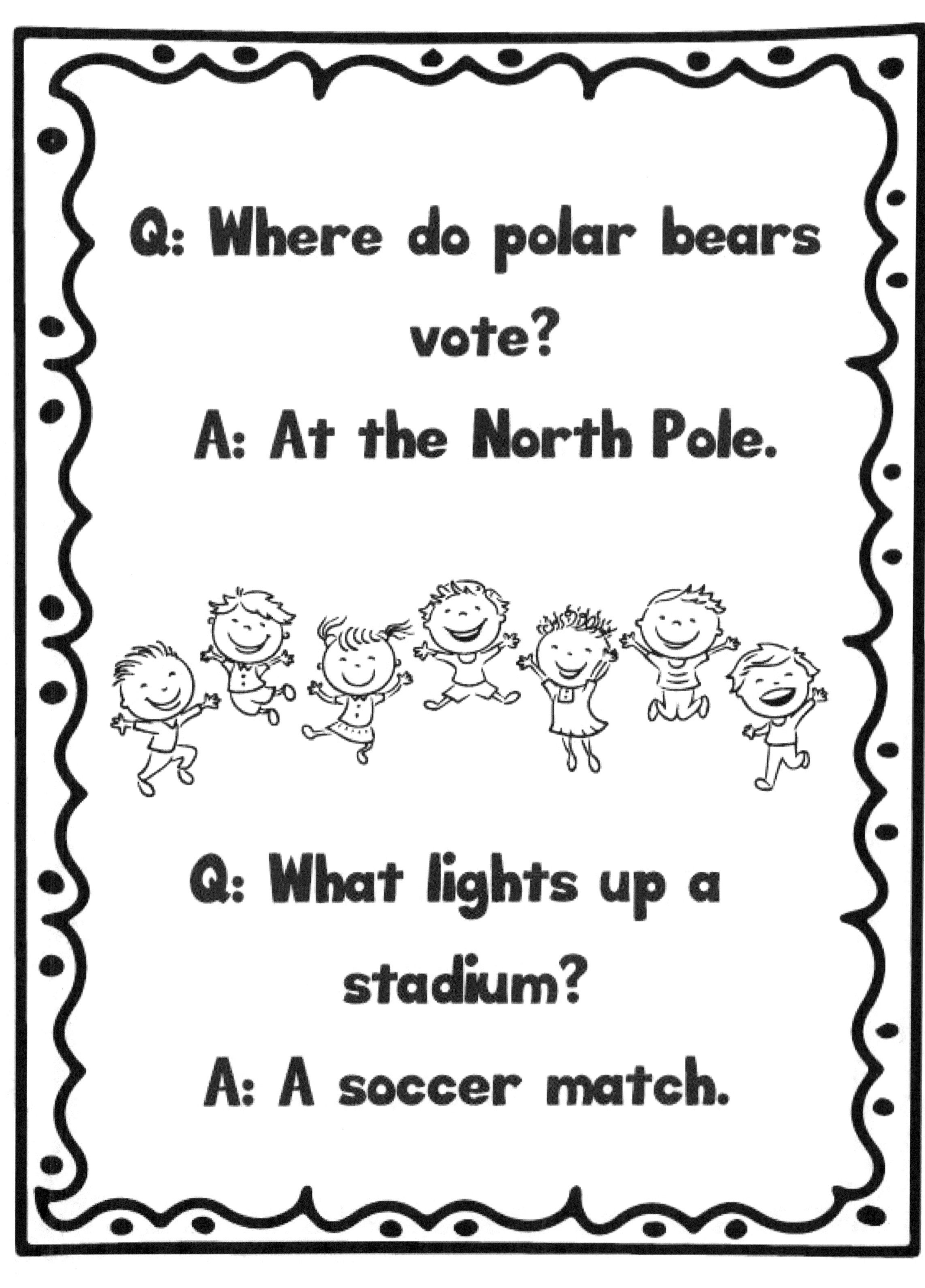
Q: Where do polar bears vote?
A: At the North Pole.
Q: What lights up a stadium?
A: A soccer match.

Q: Why couldn't the pirate play cards?
A: Because he was always on the deck.
Q: Why did the pony get detention?
A: Because he was horsing around.

Q: What do you get when you throw a lot of books into the ocean?
A: A title wave.

Q: Why did the chicken go to jail?
A: Because he was using fowl language.

Q: What has two legs but can't walk?

A: A pair of pants.

Q: What has four wheels and flies?

A: A trash truck.

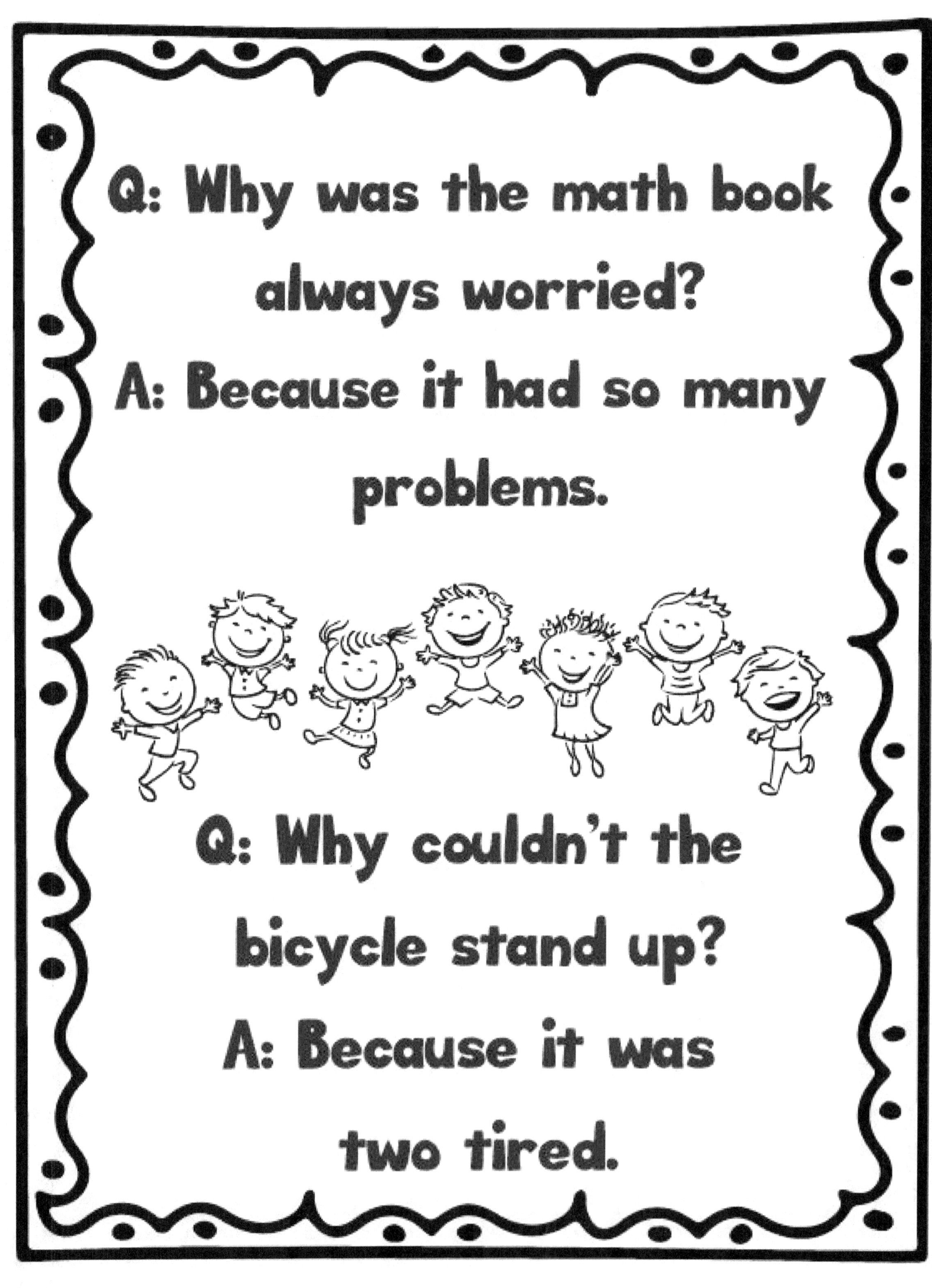

Q: Why was the math book always worried?

A: Because it had so many problems.

Q: Why couldn't the bicycle stand up?

A: Because it was two tired.

Q: What do you call a boomerang that doesn't come back?

A: A stick.

Q: Which school supply is king of the classroom?

A: The ruler.

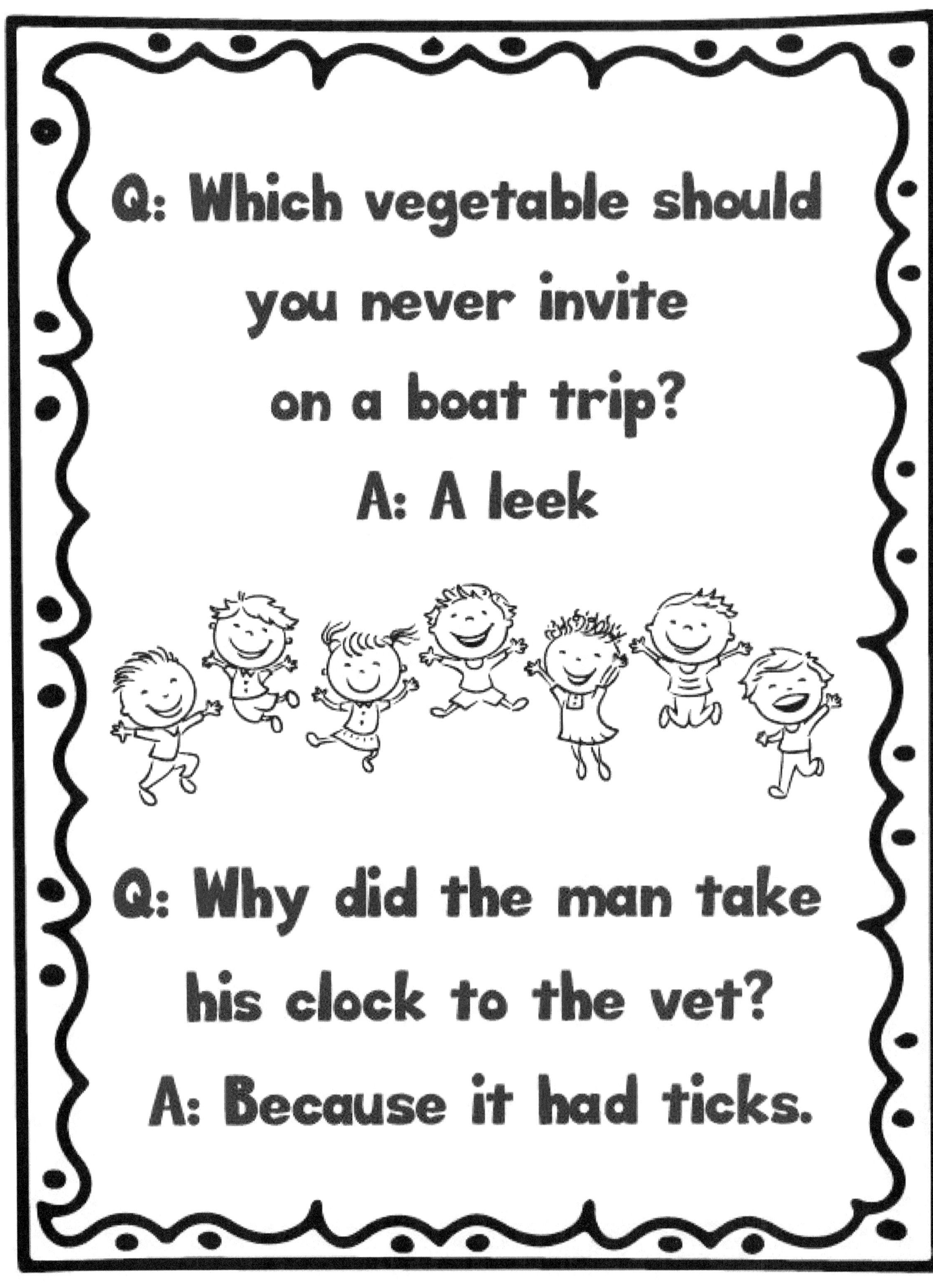

Q: Which vegetable should you never invite on a boat trip?
A: A leek
Q: Why did the man take his clock to the vet?
A: Because it had ticks.

Q: Why did the horse chew with his mouth open?

A: Because he had bad stable manners.

Q: How did Benjamin Franklin feel when he discovered electricity?

A: He was shocked.

Q: What did the mouse say to the other mouse when he tried to steal his cheese?
A: That's nacho cheese.

Q: What's a tornado's favorite game to play?
A: Twister

Q: Which is faster,
heat or cold?

A: Heat, because you can
catch a cold.

Q: What do you give
a sick lemon?

A: Lemon-aid.

Q: Why did the robber take a shower?
A: Because he wanted to make a clean getaway

Q: What's a ghost's favorite fruit?
A: Boo-berries.

Q: What did the mayonnaise say when the refrigerator was opened?
A: Close the door! I'm dressing!
Q: What do you call a shoe made from a banana?
A: A slipper.

Q: What's bigger than an elephant, but doesn't weigh anything?

A: His shadow.

Q: What did the apple tree say to the farmer?

A: Stop picking on me!

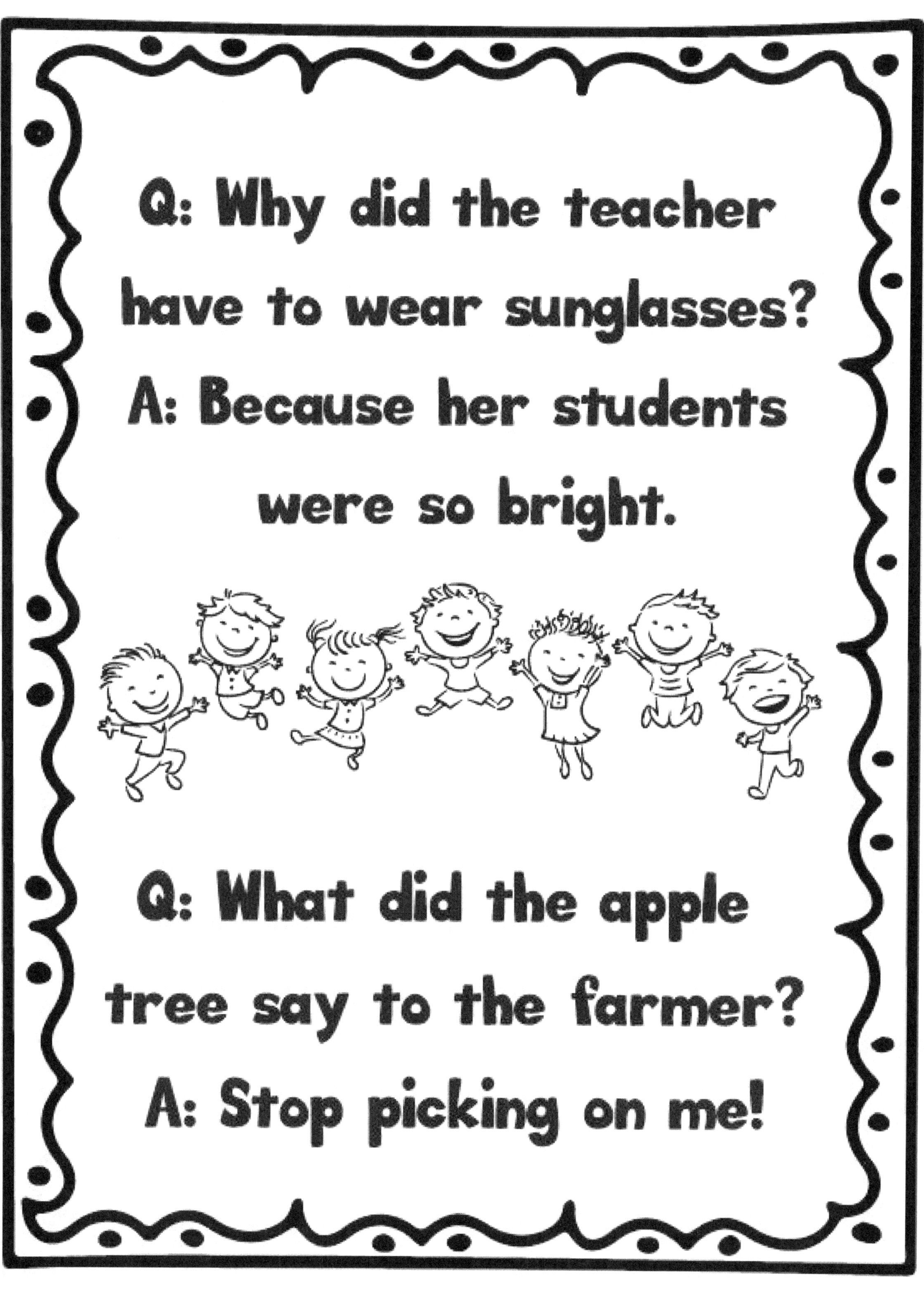

Q: Why did the teacher have to wear sunglasses?
A: Because her students were so bright.
Q: What did the apple tree say to the farmer?
A: Stop picking on me!

Q: Why are there fences around cemeteries?

A: Because people are dying to get in.

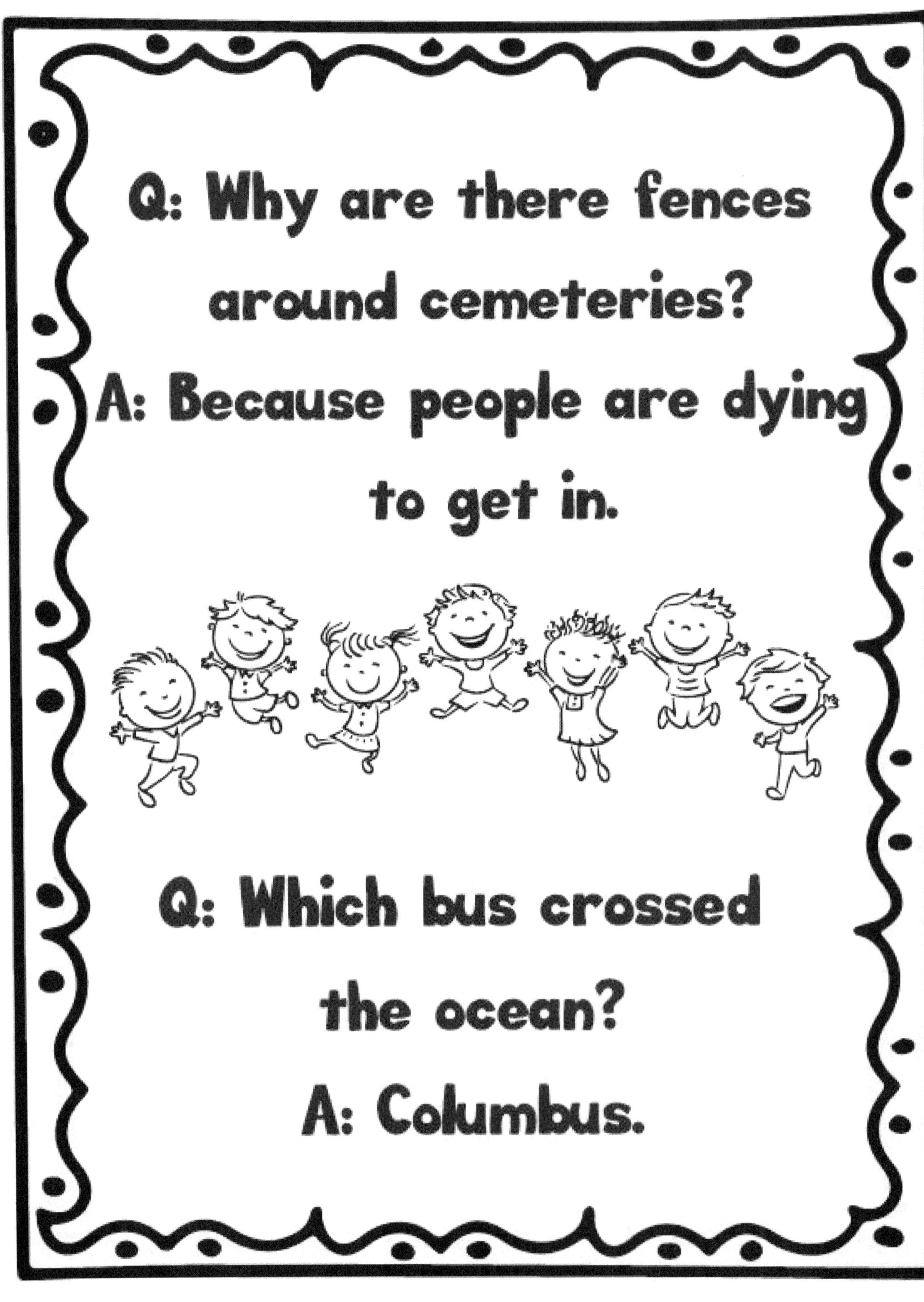

Q: Which bus crossed the ocean?

A: Columbus.

What do you call a pig
that does karate?
A: A pork chop.

Q: Where do cows go on
the weekend?
A: To the moo-vies.

Q: How do monsters tell their fortunes?
A: They read their horror-scopes.

Q: What do you call a fish with no eye?
A: A fsh.

Q: What do gymnasts, acrobats, and bananas all have in common?
A: They can all do splits.
Q: Where does the witch park her vehicle?
A: In the broom closet.

Knock, knock.

Who's there?

Yukon.

Yukon who?

Yukon a let us in?

It's raining out here!

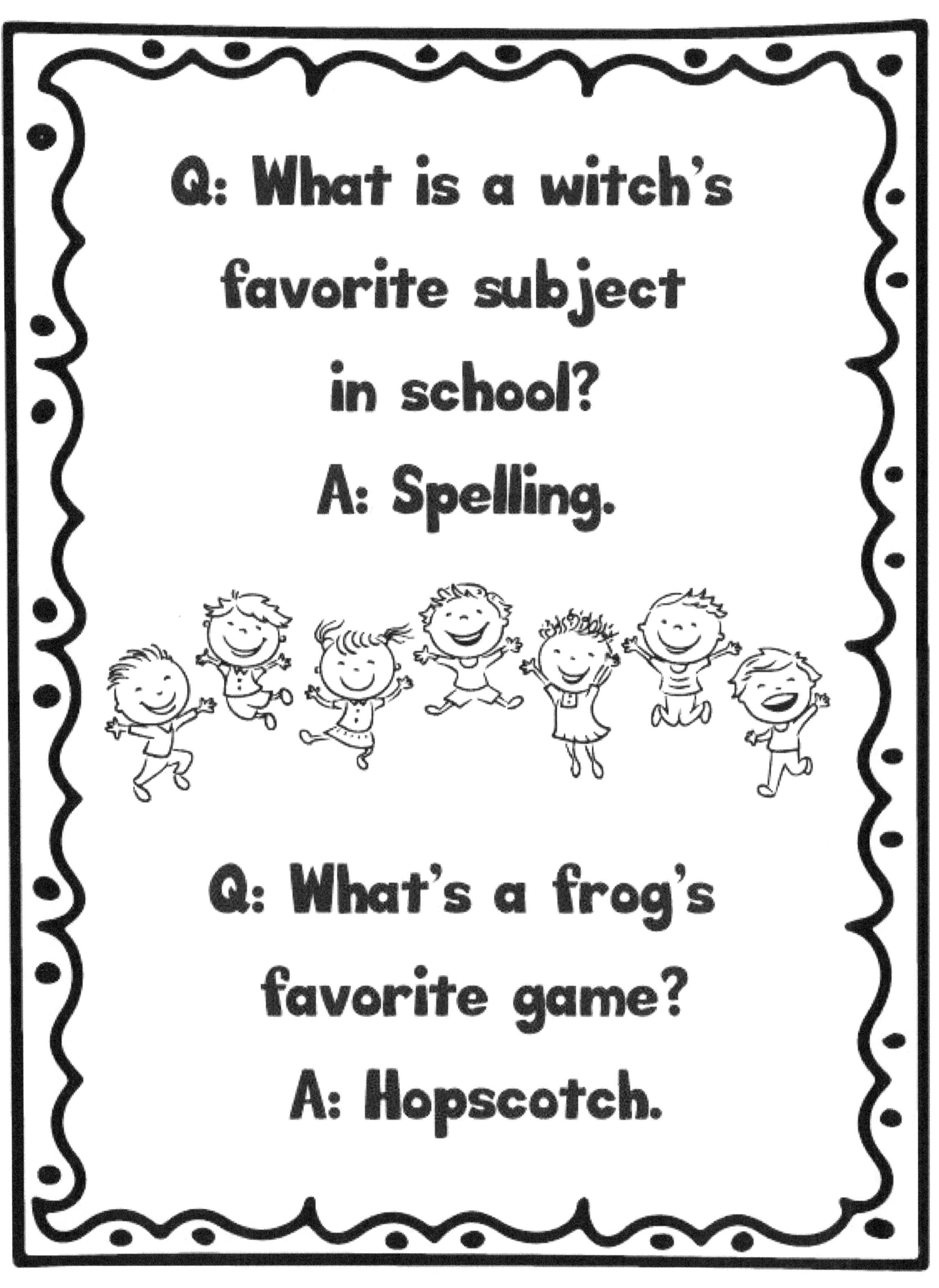
Q: What is a witch's
favorite subject
in school?
A: Spelling.
Q: What's a frog's
favorite game?
A: Hopscotch.

Q: Why couldn't the ghost see his parents?
A: Because they were trans-parents.
Q: What dies but never lives?
A: A battery

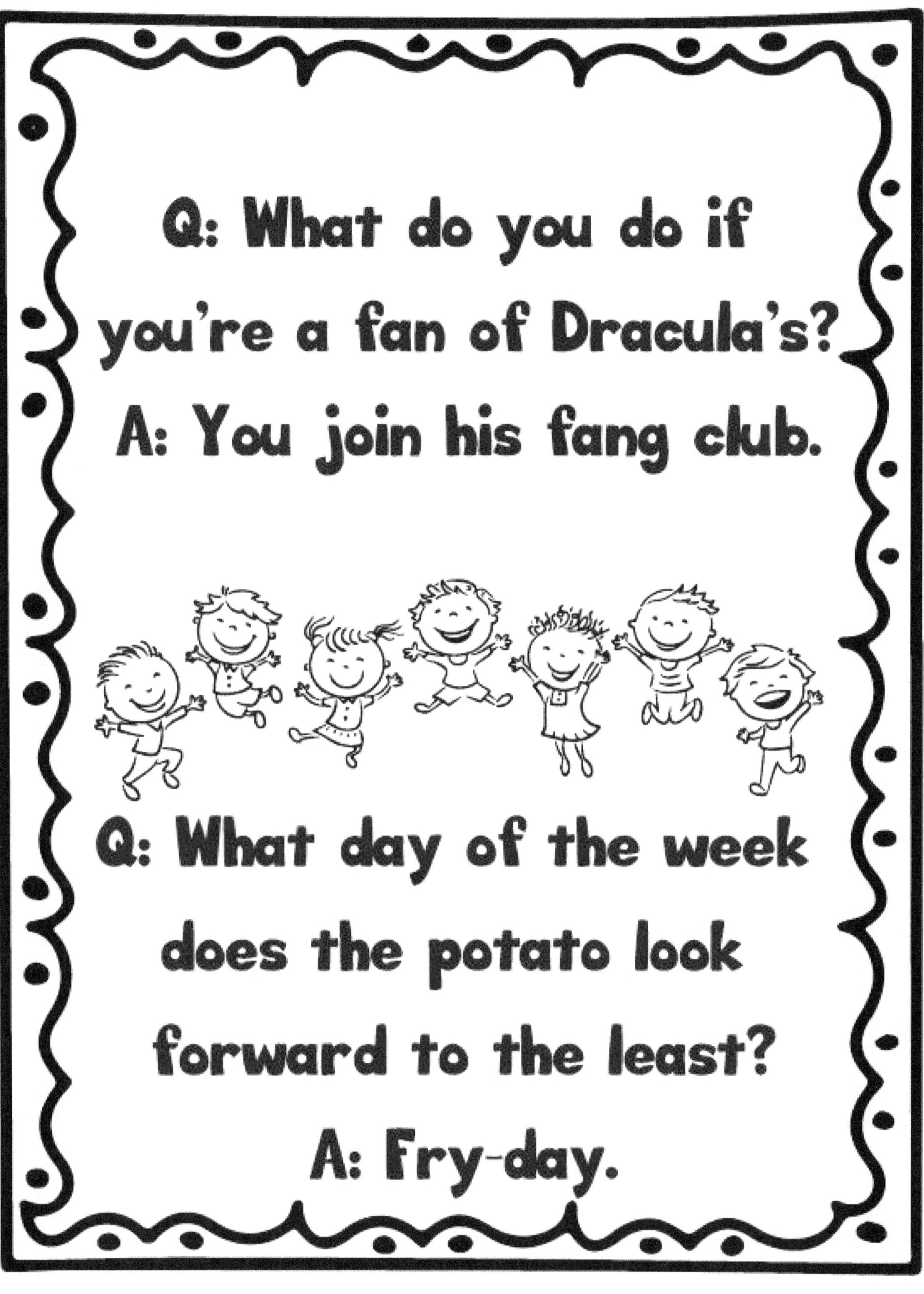

Q: What do you do if you're a fan of Dracula's?

A: You join his fang club.

Q: What day of the week does the potato look forward to the least?

A: Fry-day.

Q: What do you call a seagull that flies over the bay?
A: A bagel.
Q: What is Dracula's favorite fruit?
A: Neck-tarines.

Q: What does a skeleton
order for dinner?
A: Spare ribs.

Q: What's a ghost's
favorite dessert?
A: Ice Scream.

Q: Whom did the monster ask to kiss his boo-boos after he fell?
A: His mummy

Q: Where do ghosts go for a swim?
A: The Dead Sea.

Q: What makes a skeleton laugh?
A: When something tickles his funny bone.
Q: Why was six afraid of seven?
A: Because seven eight nine.

Q: What would you get if you crossed a teacher with a vampire?

A: Lots of blood tests.

Q: Why did the skeleton cross the road?

A: To get to the body shop.

Q: Why did the Cyclops stop teaching?

A: Because he only had one pupil.

Q: Why didn't Dracula have any friends?

A: Because he was a pain in the neck.

Knock, knock.
Who's there?
Arthur.
Arthur who?
Arthur anymore
chocolates left?

Q: Where did the witch
have to go
when she misbehaved?
A: To her broom.

Q: What do you get if you
cross a vampire and a
snowman?
A: Frostbite.

Q: What's a ghost's favorite room in the house?

A: The living room.

Q: What do birds do on Halloween?

A: They go trick or tweeting.

Q: Which monster is the best dance partner?
A: The Boogie Man.
Q: What did the turkey stay before it was roasted?
A: I'm stuffed!

Q: Why was the turkey arrested?

A: It was suspected of fowl play.

Q: What smells the best at Thanksgiving?

A: Your nose.

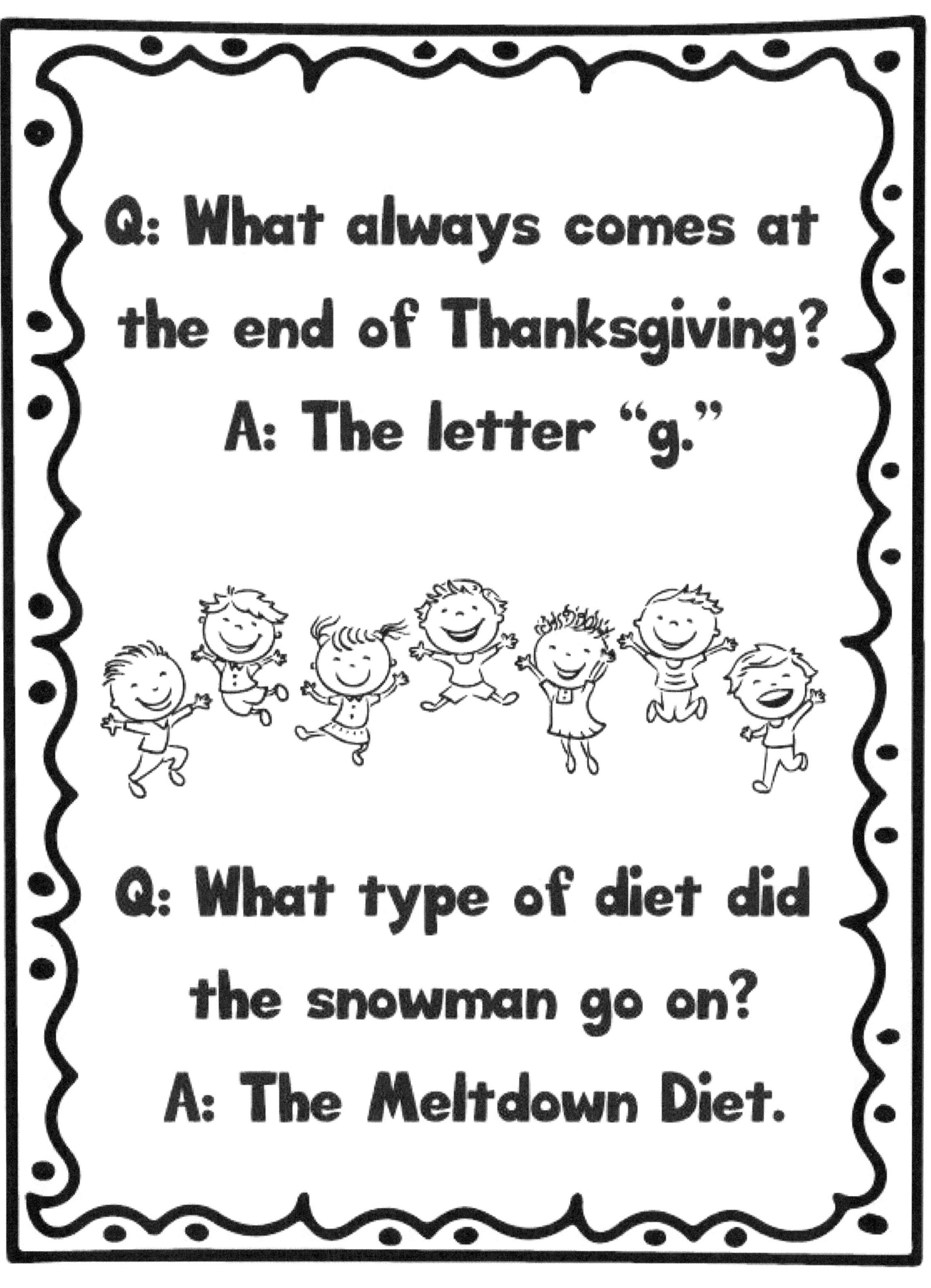

Q: What always comes at the end of Thanksgiving?
A: The letter "g."
Q: What type of diet did the snowman go on?
A: The Meltdown Diet.

Q: What do you have in December that you don't have in any other month?
A: The letter "d."
Q: What did the snowman have for breakfast?
A: Frosted Flakes

Q: Why did the boy keep his trumpet in the freezer?

A: Because he liked cool music.

Q: What often falls in winter, but never gets hurt?

A: Snow.

Q: What's the difference between a Christmas alphabet and the regular alphabet?
A: The Christmas alphabet has Noel.

Q: What's brown and sneaks around the kitchen?
A: Mince spies.

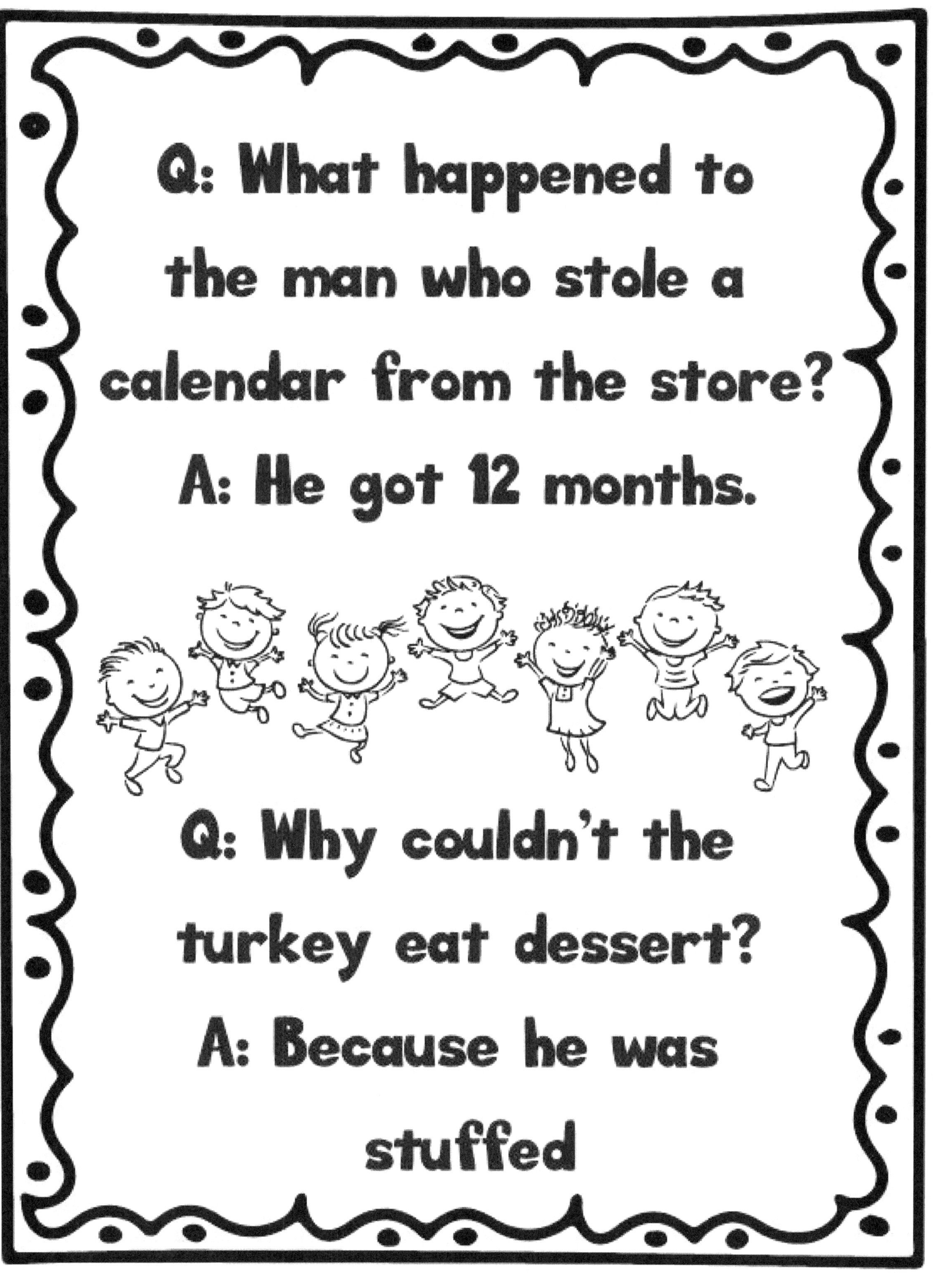

Q: What happened to the man who stole a calendar from the store?
A: He got 12 months.
Q: Why couldn't the turkey eat dessert?
A: Because he was stuffed

Knock, knock.
Who's there?
Needle.
Needle who?
Needle little more money
for this toy please.

Q: What type of key is the most important at Thanksgiving dinner?

A: The tur-key.

Q: Which side of the turkey has the most feathers?

A: The outside.

Q: Are turkey leftovers good for your health?
A: Not if you're the turkey!
Q: What do elves learn in school?
A: The elf-abet.

Q: What do you get if you cross a pinetree with an apple?
A: A pine-apple.
Q: Why was Santa's helper sad?
A: Because he had low elf-esteem.

Q: What does Santa clean
his sleigh with?
A: Comet.

Q: What did the stamp
say to the envelope?
A: I'm stuck on you.

Q: What did the paper clip say to the magnet?
A: I find you very attractive.
Q: What kind of flower do you never want to get on Valentine's Day?
A: Cauliflower.

Q: What do elephants say to one another on Valentine's Day?
A: I love you a ton.

Q: What's easy to get into, but hard to get out of?
A: Trouble.

Q: What has an eye, but cannot see?

A: A needle (or potato, tornado, hurricane, etc.).

Q: Why is the forest so noisy?

A: Because the trees have bark.

Q: If a butcher wears a size XL shirt and a size 13 shoe, what does he weigh?
A: Meat.
Q: What did the baker say to his wife?
A: I'm dough-nuts about you!

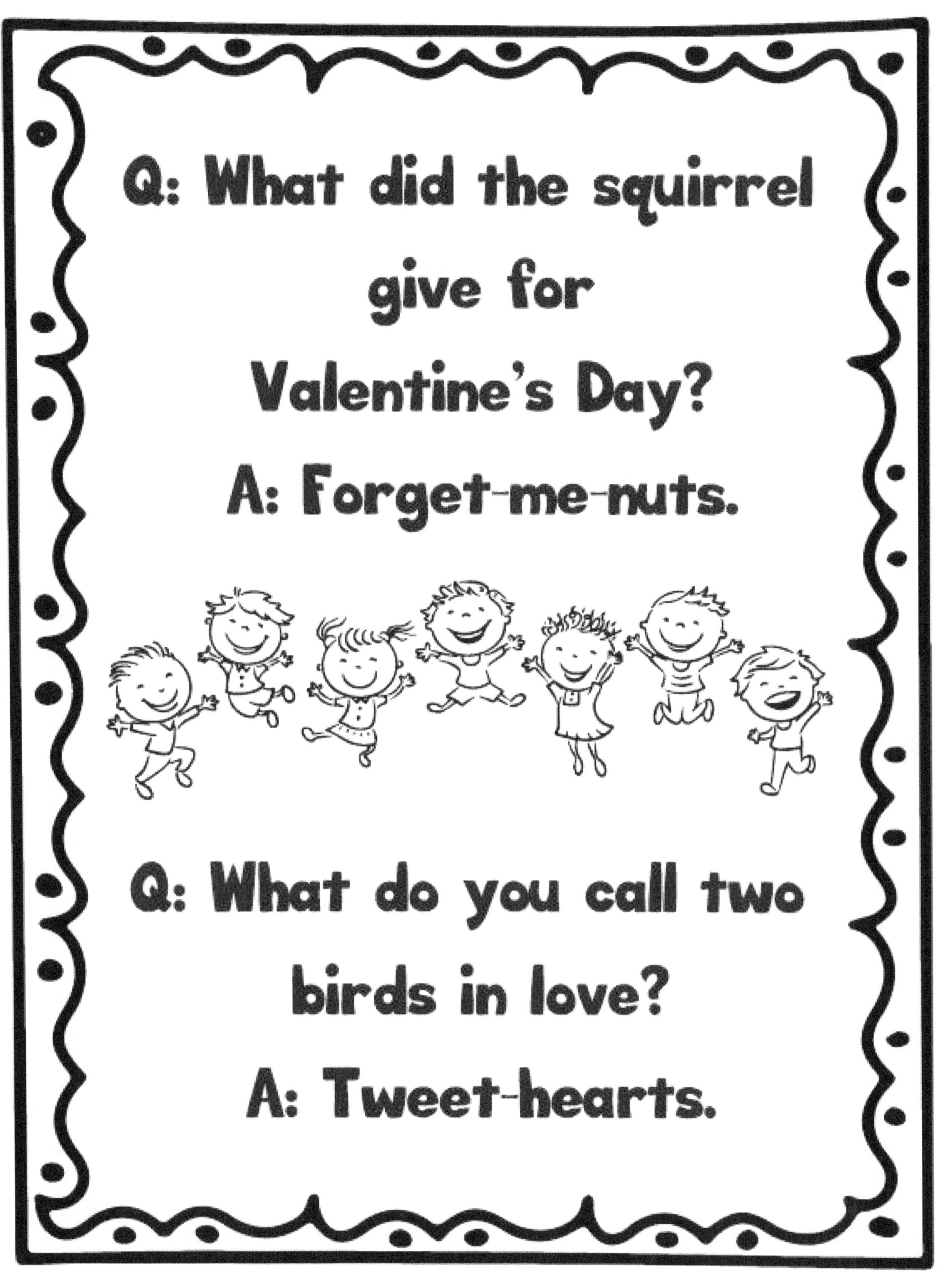

Q: What did the squirrel give for Valentine's Day?

A: Forget-me-nuts.

Q: What do you call two birds in love?

A: Tweet-hearts.

Knock, knock.
Who's there?
Canoe.
Canoe who?
Canoe help me with
my homework please?

Q: What did the monster ask his sweetheart?
A: Will you be my Valen-slime?
Q: What did the boy pickle say to the girl pickle?
A: You mean a great dill to me.

Q: What did the farmer give his wife for Valentine's Day?
A: Hogs and kisses.
Q: What did the owl say to his sweetheart?
A: Owl be yours.

Q: What did the snowman order at Wendy's®?
A: A Frosty!

Q: Why can't skeletons play music?
A: Because they have no organs.

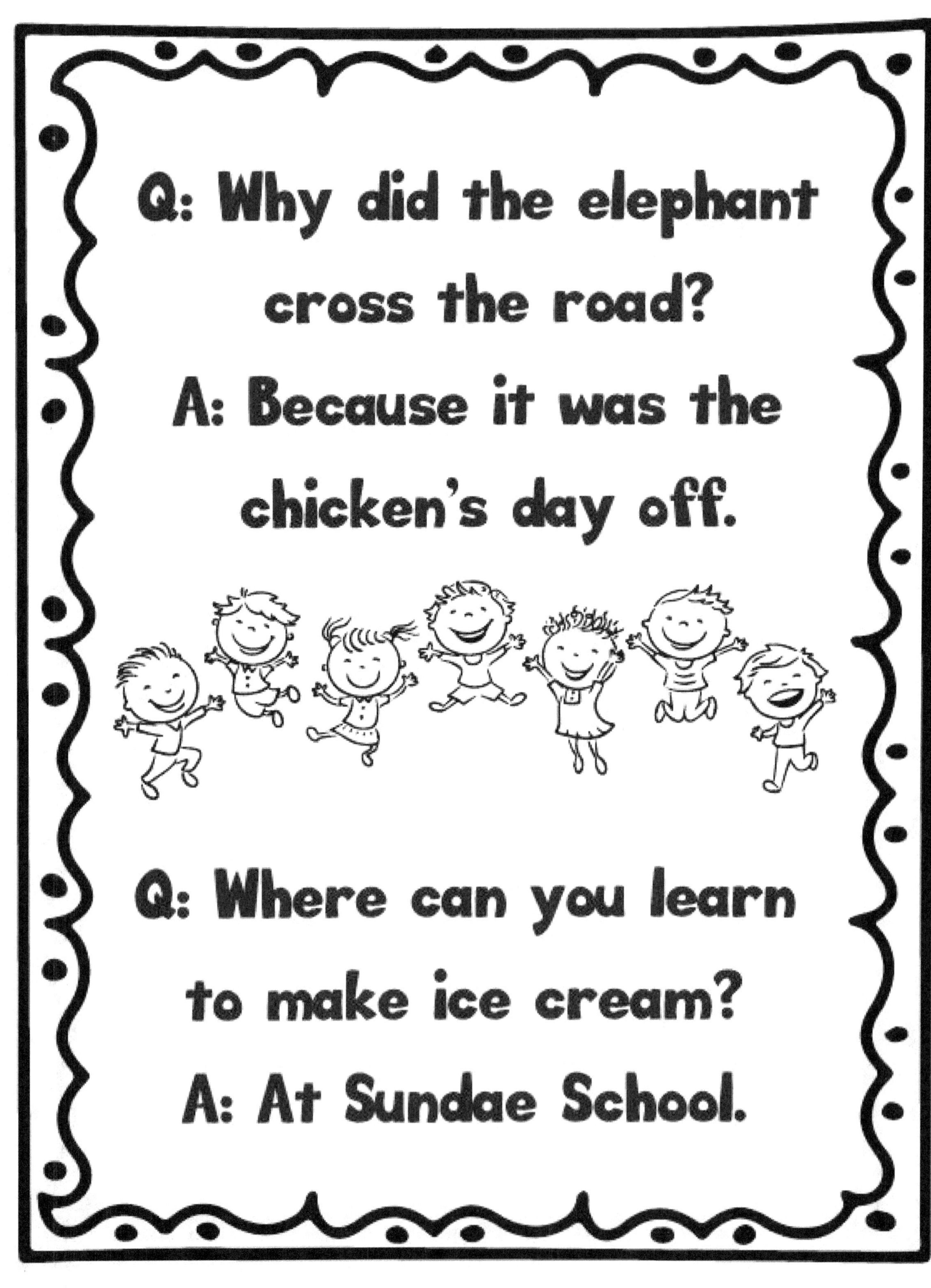

Q: Why did the elephant cross the road?

A: Because it was the chicken's day off.

Q: Where can you learn to make ice cream?

A: At Sundae School.

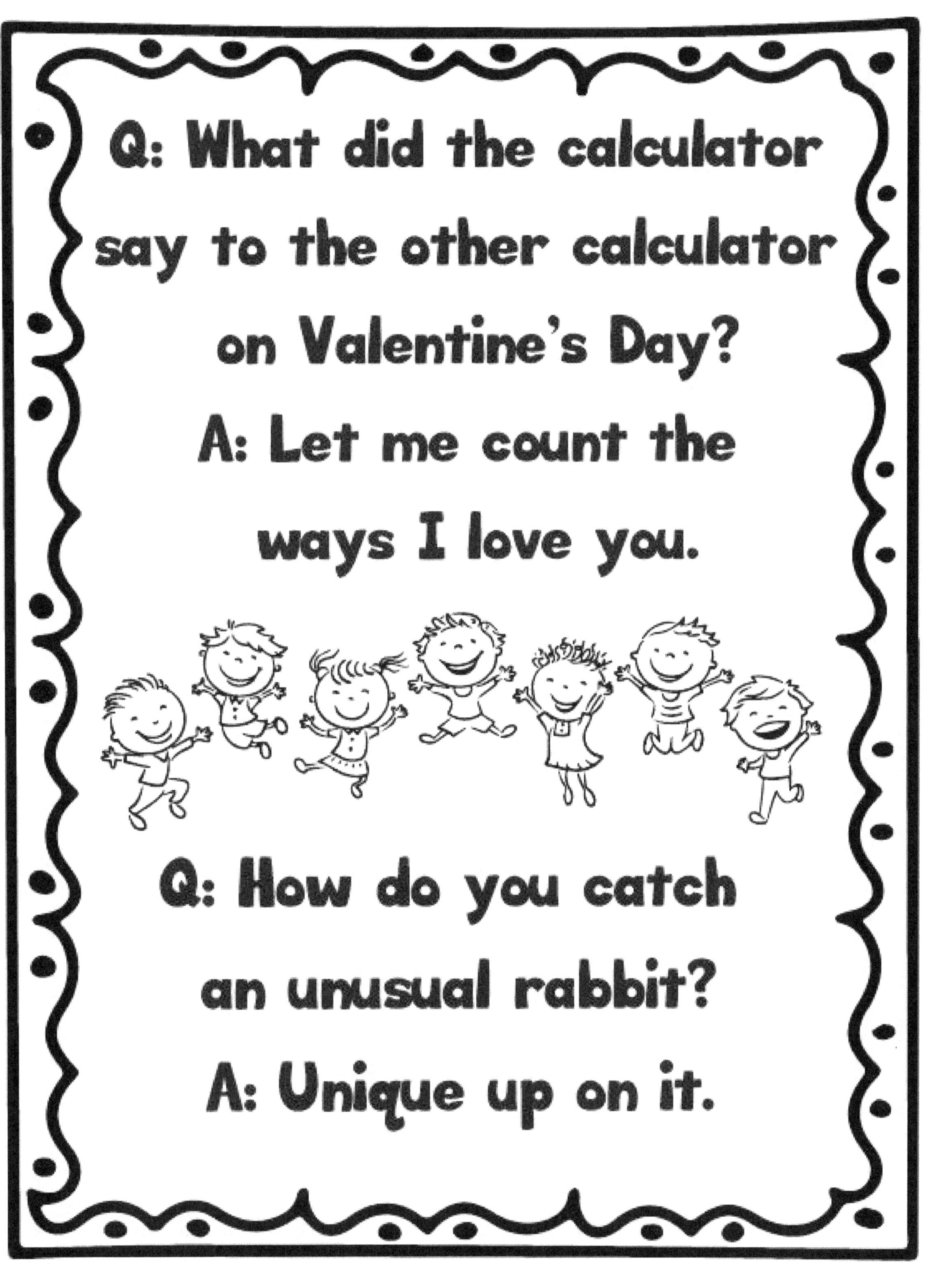

Q: What did the calculator say to the other calculator on Valentine's Day?
A: Let me count the ways I love you.
Q: How do you catch an unusual rabbit?
A: Unique up on it.

Q: Why did the boy run around his bed?
A: He was trying to catch up on his sleep.
Q: What do you call an elephant in a phone booth?
A: Stuck!

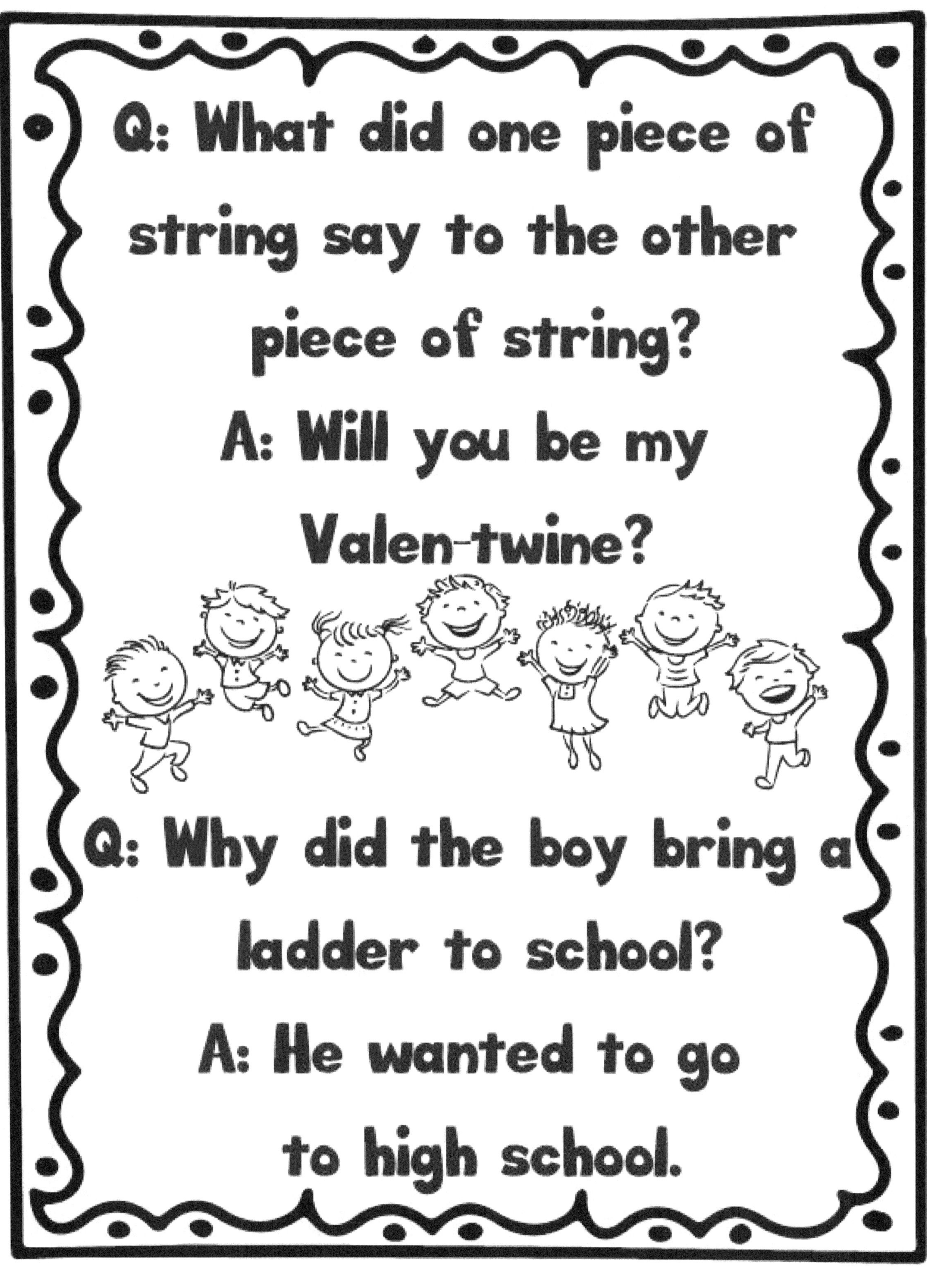

Q: What did one piece of string say to the other piece of string?
A: Will you be my Valen-twine?
Q: Why did the boy bring a ladder to school?
A: He wanted to go to high school.

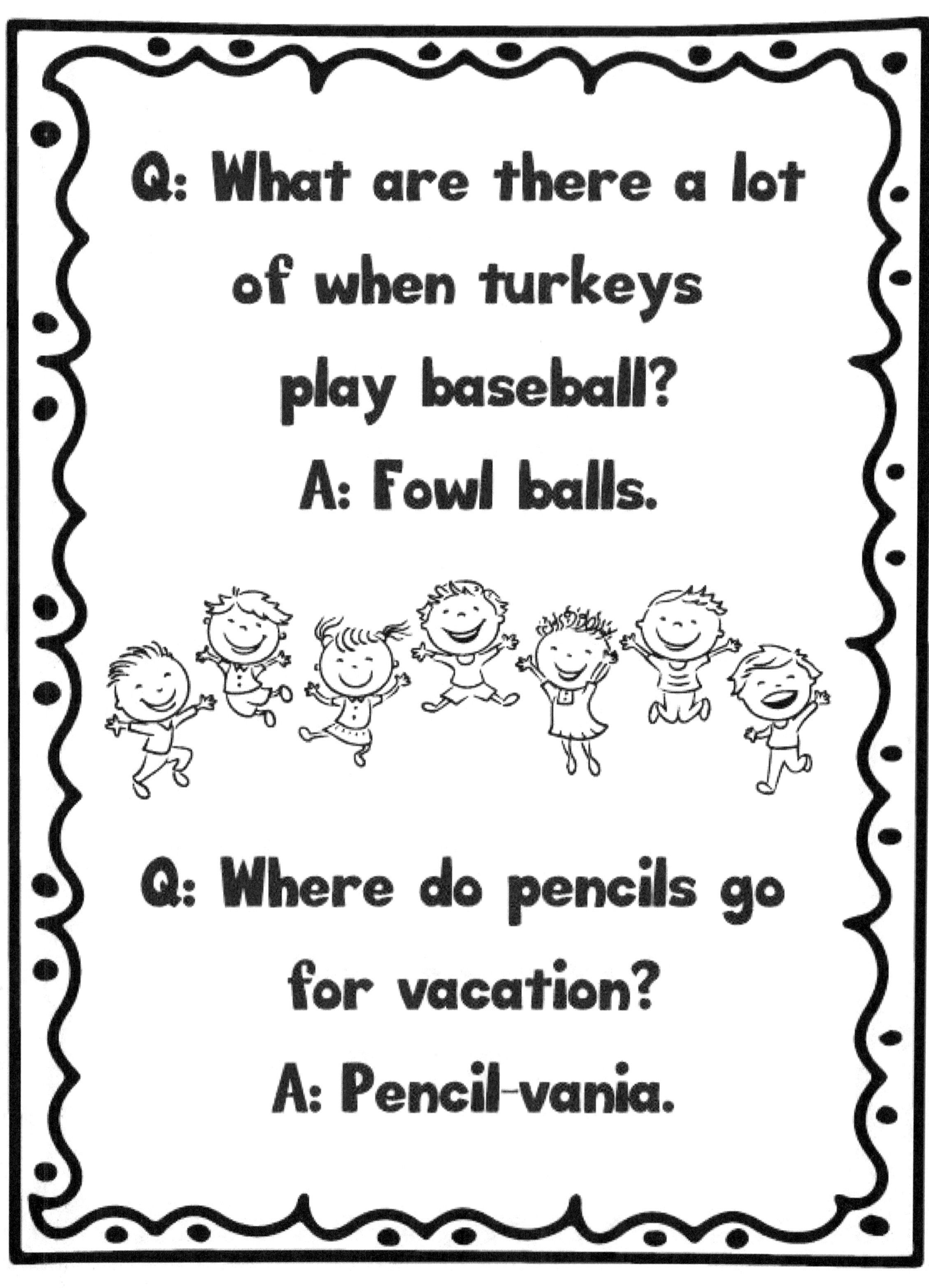

Q: What are there a lot of when turkeys play baseball?
A: Fowl balls.
Q: Where do pencils go for vacation?
A: Pencil-vania.

Q: How does the Easter Bunny travel?
A: By hare-plane.
Q: What runs but never walks?
A: A hose.

Knock, knock.
Who's there?
Nobel.
Nobel who?
There's nobel,
that's why I'm knocking.

Q: Which flower talks the most?
A: Tulips, because they have two lips.
Q: What did the spoon say to the knife?
A: "You're so sharp!"

Q: How did the hairdresser win the race?

A: She knew a shortcut.

Q: Why are fish so smart?

A: Because they are always in a school.

Q: What did the dinner plate say to the cup?
A: Dinner's on me tonight.
Q: What did the circle say to the triangle?
A: I don't see your point.

Q: What's black and white over and over again?
A: A penguin rolling down a hill.

Q: What's a rabbit's favorite kind of music?
A: Hip-hop.

Q: Where's a wall's favorite place tomeet his friends?

A: At the corner.

Q: Where did the king keep his army?

A: In his sleeve.

Q: Why don't animals eat clowns?
A: They taste funny!
Q: Where do books hide when they're scared?
A: Under their covers.

Q: What's a scarecrow's favorite fruit?
A: Strawberries.
Q: Why can't the elephant use the computer?
A: Because he's afraid of the mouse.

Q: What do a car and an elephant have in common?

A: They both have trunks.

Q: Why do cowboys ride horses?

A: Because they're too heavy to carry.

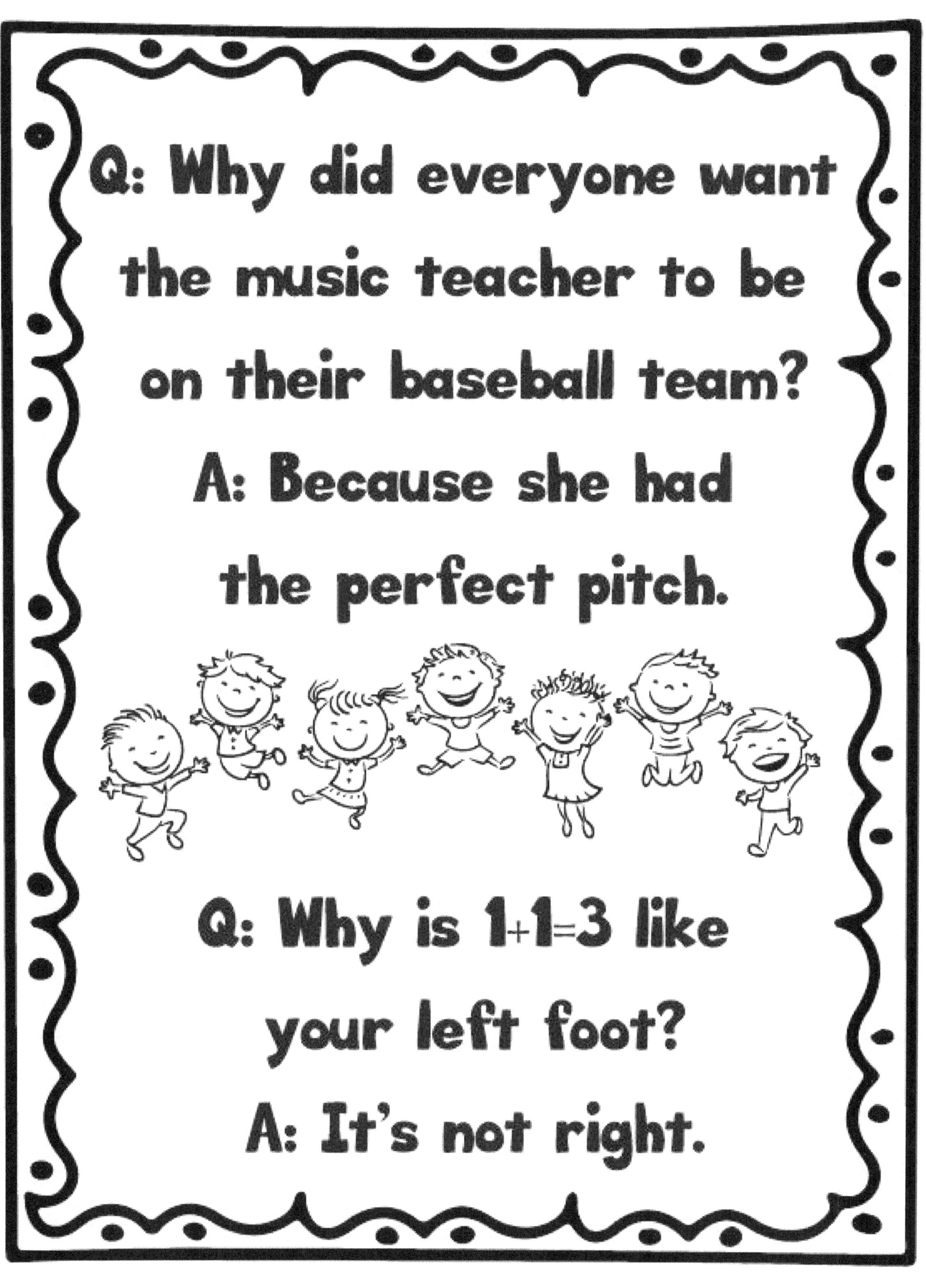

Q: Why did everyone want the music teacher to be on their baseball team?
A: Because she had the perfect pitch.
Q: Why is 1+1=3 like your left foot?
A: It's not right.

Knock, knock.
Who's there?
Pecan.
Pecan who?
Pecan someone
your own size!

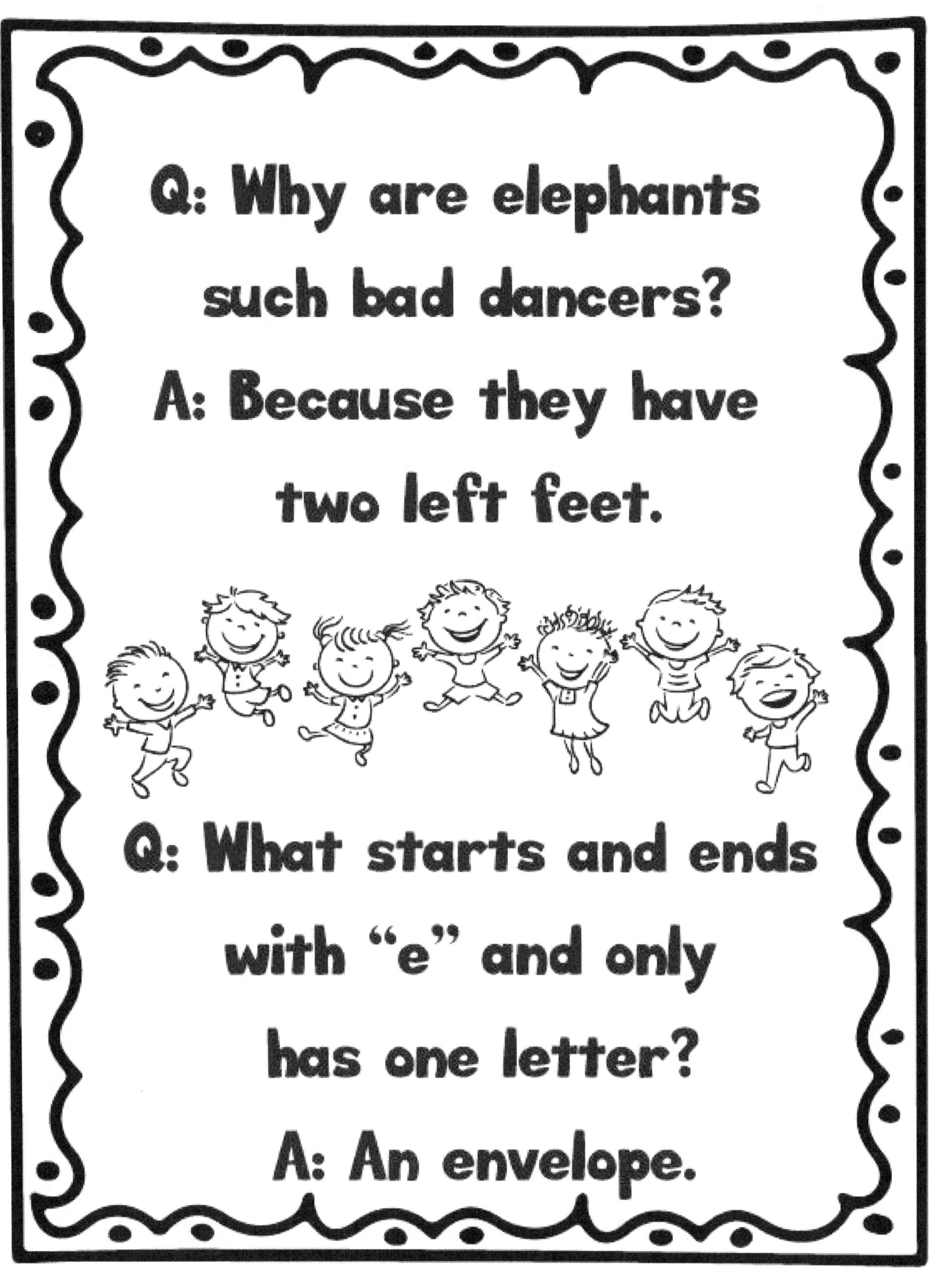

Q: Why are elephants such bad dancers?

A: Because they have two left feet.

Q: What starts and ends with "e" and only has one letter?

A: An envelope.

Q: What should you do if your teacher rolls her eyes at you?
A: Roll them back, of course!
Q: What's a math teacher's favorite tool?
A: Multipliers.

Q: Why didn't the oven go to college?

A: Because it had a lot of degrees already

Q: Why do bees have sticky hair?

A: Because they have honeycombs.

Q: What did the teacher do at the beach?

A: She tested the water

Q: What time is it when you have a toothache?

A: Tooth Hurty

Q: How did the boy react when his turtle died?
A: He was shell-shocked.

Q: What's a spider's favorite thing to do on a computer?
A: Make websites.

Q: What's a librarian's favorite type of bait when fishing?
A: Bookworms.

Q: What kind of table can you have for dinner?
A: A vege-table.

Q: Why did the girl put lipstick on her head?

A: Because she wanted to make-up her mind

Q: What did one eye say to the other?

A: Between you and I, something smells.

Q: What did the ocean
say to the beach?
A: Nothing,
it just waved.

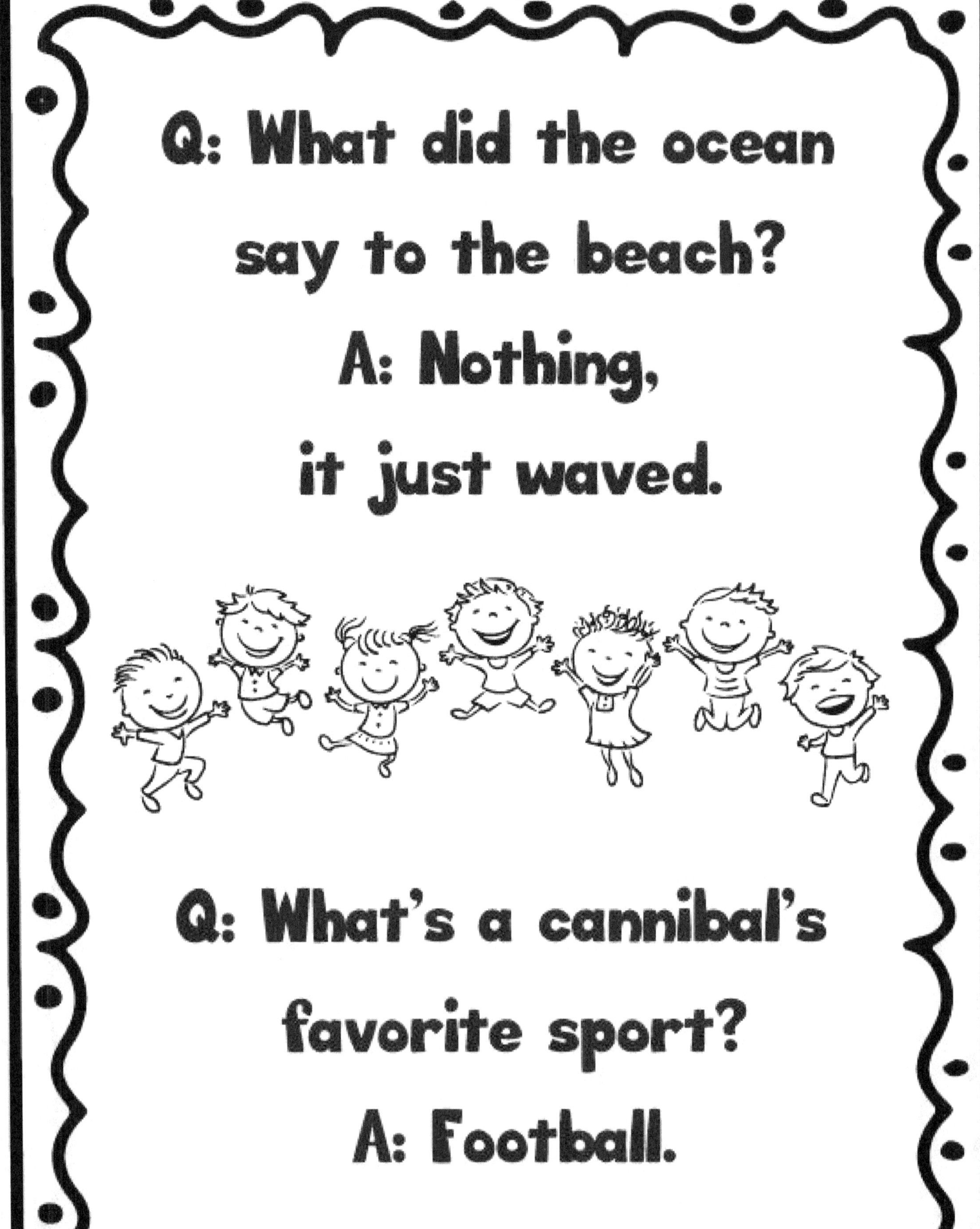

Q: What's a cannibal's
favorite sport?
A: Football.

Q: Why was the computer cold?
A: Because it left the Windows open!
Q: What do you call a worm with no teeth?
A: A gummy worm.

Knock, knock.
Who's there?
Cows go.
Cows go who?
No, silly, cows go MOO!

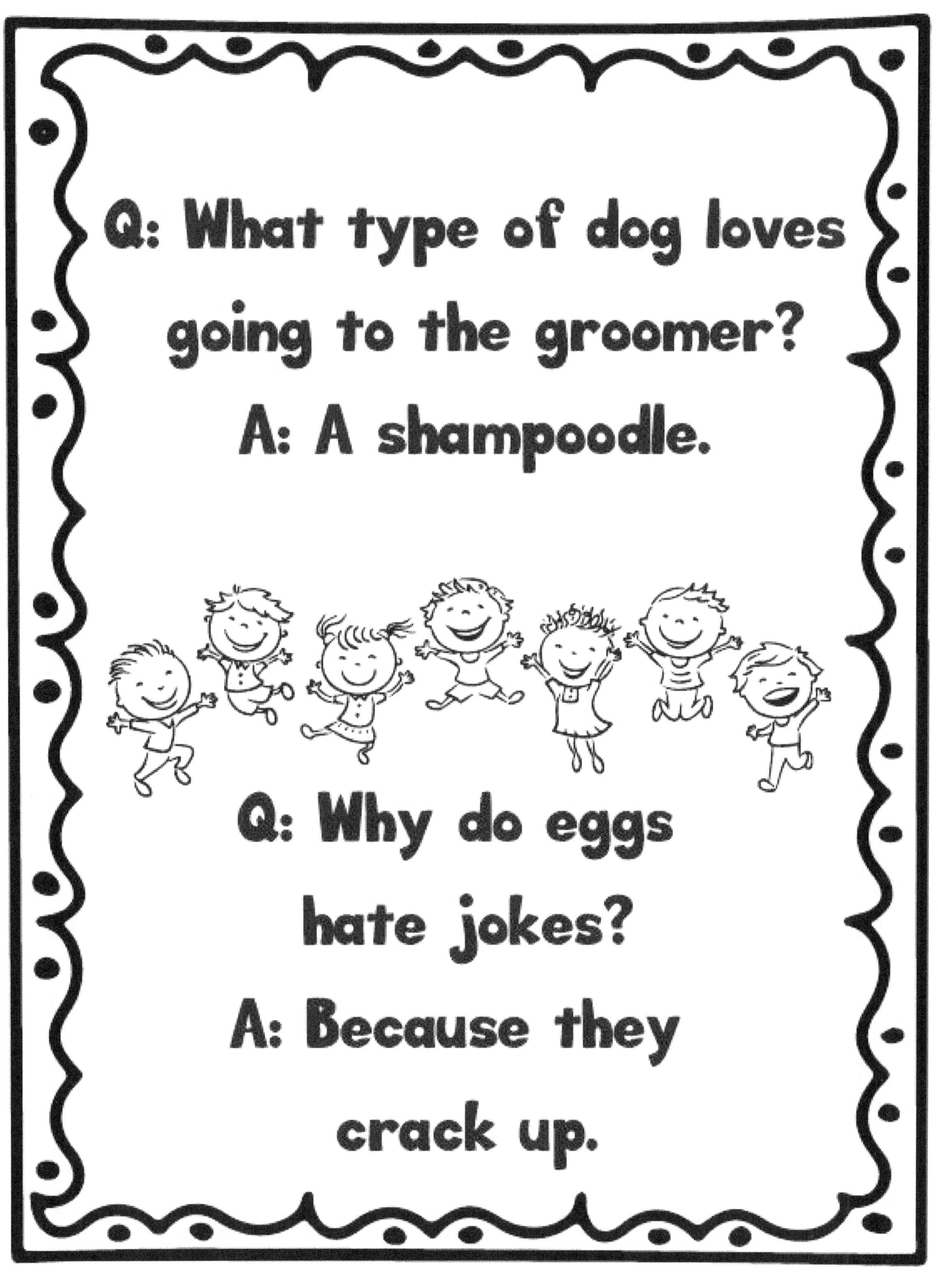

Q: What type of dog loves going to the groomer?
A: A shampoodle.
Q: Why do eggs hate jokes?
A: Because they crack up.

Q: What did the doctor diagnose the horse with when he wasn't feeling well?

A: Hay fever.

Q: Why do birds fly south for the winter?

A: Because it's too far to walk.

Q: What lies at the bottom
of the ocean and worries?
A: A nervous wreck.

Q: What's the smartest
insect around?
A: The spelling bee.

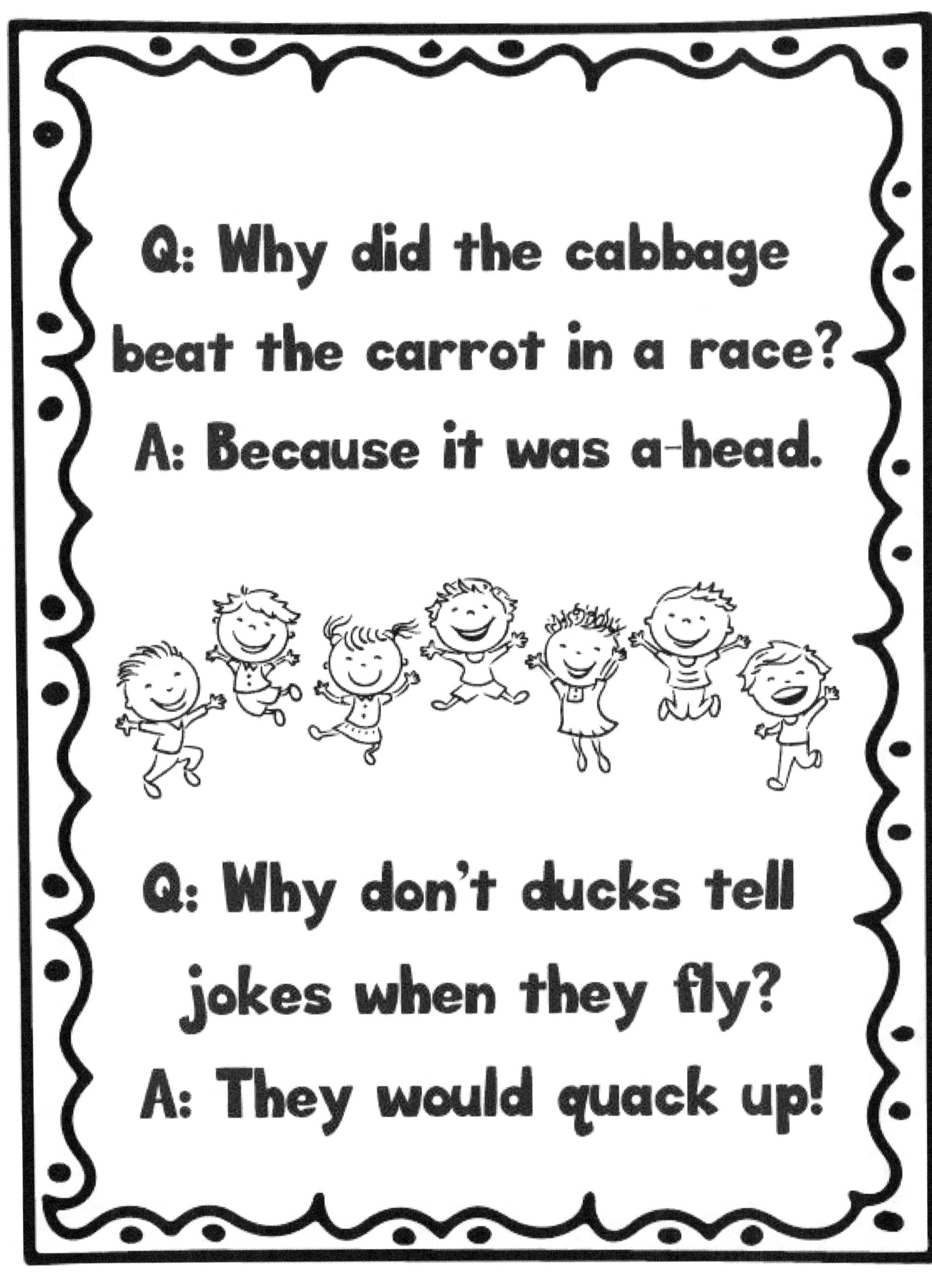

Q: Why did the cabbage beat the carrot in a race?
A: Because it was a-head.
Q: Why don't ducks tell jokes when they fly?
A: They would quack up!

Q: What's a bat's favorite pastime?
A: Hanging out with his friends.

Q: Where do polar bears keep their money?
A: In snow banks.

Knock, knock.
Who's there?
Leaf.
Leaf who?
Leaf me alone please,
I'm thinking.

Knock, knock.

Who's there?

Cash.

Cash who?

No, thanks, I prefer peanuts.

Q: How do bears keep their den cool in the summer?

A: They use bear-conditioning.

Q: Why was the clown crying?

A: Because he broke his funny bone.

Q: What did the paper say to encourage the pencil?
A: Write on, good friend!
Q: Where can you always find a peacock?
A: In the dictionary.

Knock, knock.
Who's there?
Tank.
Tank who?
You're welcome!

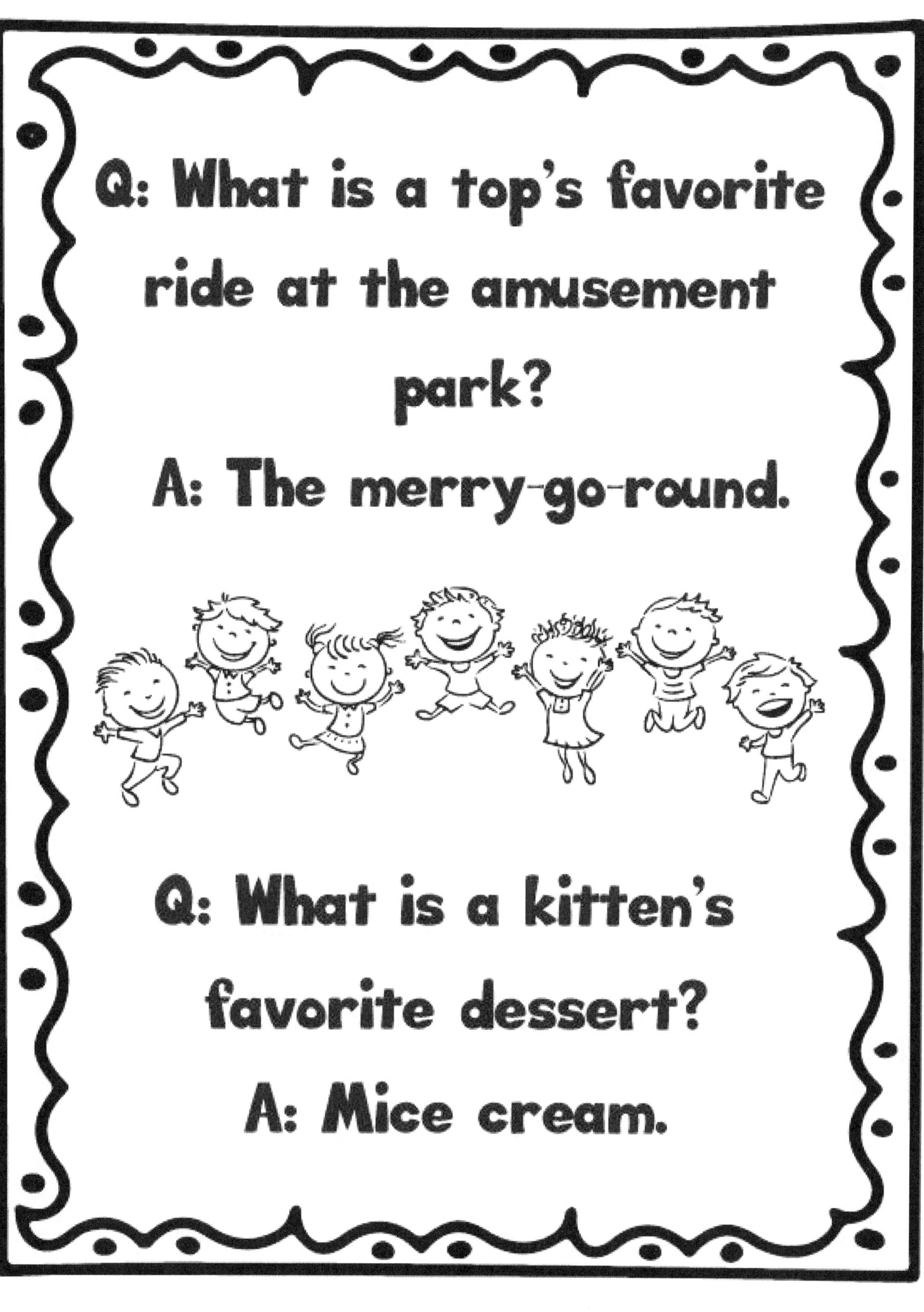

Q: What is a top's favorite ride at the amusement park?

A: The merry-go-round.

Q: What is a kitten's favorite dessert?

A: Mice cream.

Q: Where did the bird go when he lost a feather?
A: The re-tail shop.
Q: What's a cat's favorite nursery rhyme?
A: Three Blind Mice.

Q: Why did the dog
keep tripping?
A: Because she had
two left feet.

Q: What did the duck say
to the clown?
A: You quack me up!

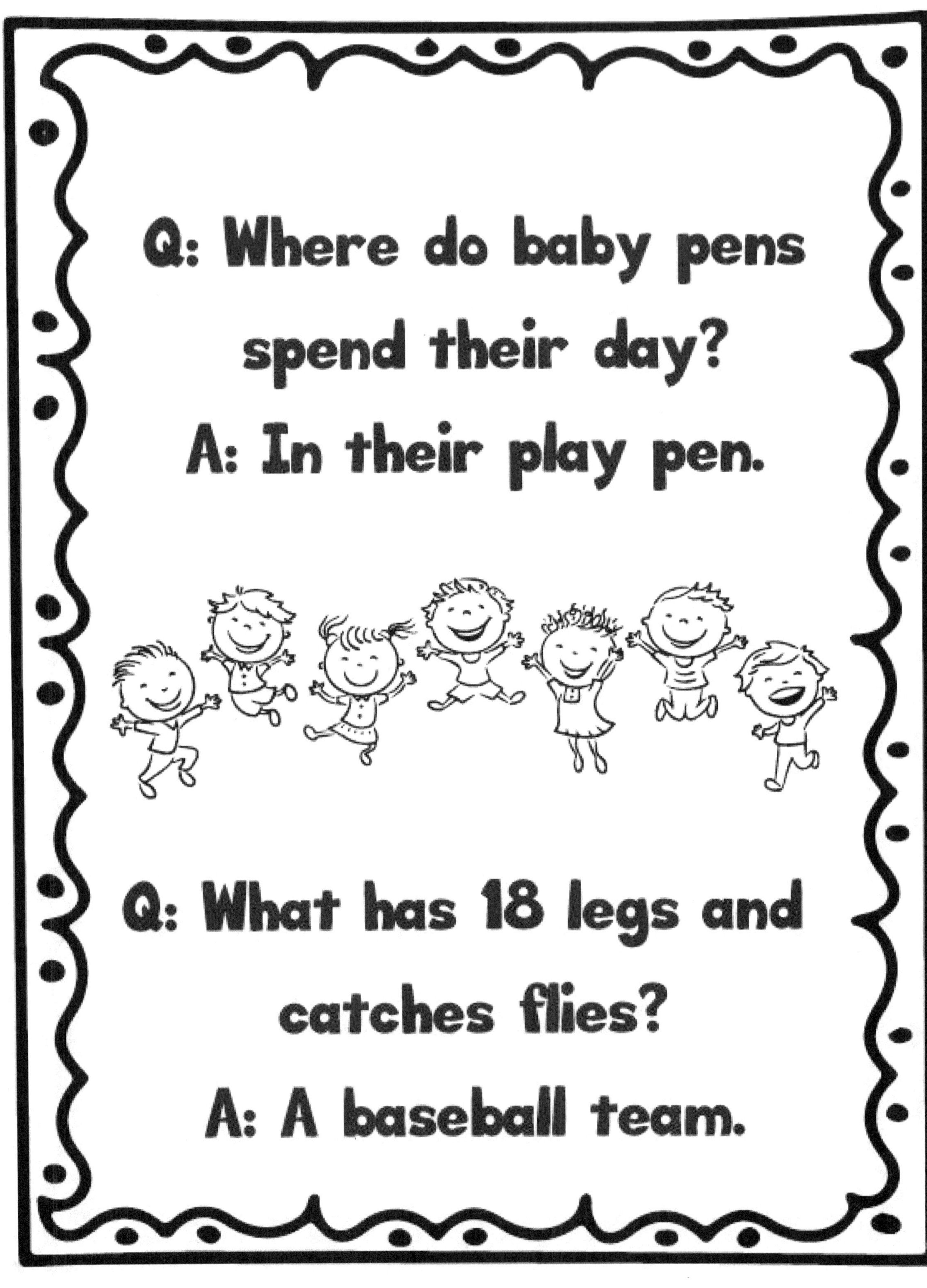

Q: Where do baby pens spend their day?

A: In their play pen.

Q: What has 18 legs and catches flies?

A: A baseball team.

Q: Why is it not a good idea to try to trick a snake?

A: Because you can't pull his leg.

Q: What was the banker's favorite player on the football team?

A: The quarterback.

Q: Why couldn't the boy go
to the pirate movie?
A: Because it was
rated "ARRR!"

Q: What bird loves
construction work?
A: A crane.

Q: What did the farmer say to the horse when he walked in the barn?
A: "Why the long face?"
Q: How long should an elephant's legs be?
A: Long enough to reach the ground.

Q: What gives you
the power to walk
through a wall?
A: A door.

Q: What do you call
a left-handed dog?
A: A south paw.

Q: What did the students do when their shoelaces got tangled together?

A: They went on a class trip.

Q: Why did the book join the police force?

A: He wanted to go undercover.

Knock, knock.
Who's there?
Who.
Who who?
Is there an owl in here?

Q: Why did the teddy bear say no to dessert?
A: Because she was stuffed.
Q: What has ears but cannot hear?
A: A cornfield.

Q: What did the left eye say to the right eye?

A: Between us, something smells!

Q: What did one plate say to the other plate?

A: Dinner is on me!

Q: Why do bananas have to put sunscreen on before they go to the beach?
A: Because they peel!

Knock, knock.
Who's there?
Banana.
Banana who?
Knock, knock.
Who's there?
Banana.
Banana who?
Knock, knock.
Who's there?
Banana.
Banana who?
Knock, knock.
Who's there?
Orange.
Orange who?
Orange you glad I didn't say banana?